For my family and friends for their endless support;
for my agency, Plum Pudding, who invested so much time and belief in me;
and finally for Rob, my partner in crime.

Sky Pony Press books may be purchased in bulk at special discounts for sales promotion, corporate gifts, fund-raising, or educational purposes. Special editions can also be created to specifications. For details, contact the Special Sales Department, Sky Pony Press, 307 West 36th Street, 11th Floor, New York, NY 10018 or info@ skyhorsepublishing.com.

Sky Pony® is a registered trademark of Skyhorse Publishing, Inc.®, a Delaware corporation.

Visit our website at www.skyponypress.com.

10 9 8 7 6 5 4 3 2 1

Manufactured in China, January 2016
This product conforms to CPSIA 2008

Library of Congress Cataloging-in-Publication Data is available on file.

Cover design and illustrations by Amy Proud

Print ISBN: 978-1-63450-174-3
Ebook ISBN: 978-1-63450-616-8

Izzy

the very bad Burglar

Amy Proud

Sky Pony Press
New York

Sunnyside Lane was dark. All was silent and still...

but if you looked closely,
   you'd see hiding in a tangly tall tree,
      a little burglar and her friend, Frog.

and even her little
cousin was a notorious
bank robber.

CRIME TIMES
WANTED

DANGEROUS
$10,000

But every time Izzy took
something that didn't belong to her,
she got a bad feeling in her stomach
that wouldn't go away.

Izzy tried to tell her parents about the bad feeling but whenever she mentioned it, they would scowl and grind their teeth and tell her she must be a good burglar.

So Izzy found ways to make the funny feeling in her stomach go away.

Whenever she burgled a house, she also did something nice for the family, hoping this would make it not quite so bad when they got home.

But after a while, the funny feeling would come back.

Then they started to make the beds and dust, wash the dishes, and do the laundry.

so when the family came home, some of their things would be gone...

but at least they wouldn't have any chores to do.

But after a while, the funny feeling would come back.

So, Izzy also started baking her special double chocolate brownies with gooey caramel chunks.

When the family realized they had been burgled, at least they would have a nice, tidy house with no chores to do and something sweet to eat.

But after a while, the funny feeling would come back.

Frog suggested that while Izzy cleaned and dusted and tidied and baked, he could do some gardening, so that when the family came home, they would have been robbed, but the house would be tidy, all the chores would be done, there'd be a table of delicious desserts to eat, and there would be new plants in the yard to cheer them up.

But after a while, the funny feeling would come back.

So, after Izzy and Frog had done all the cleaning and baking and gardening, they bathed and walked the dogs. Even though they had been burgled, when the family got home their house would be spotless, there would be plenty of treats to eat, their garden would have a stylish new fountain, and the dogs would be looking quite stunning.

(Frog was very good at giving them fancy hair styles!)

But after a while, the funny feeling would come back.

Izzy and Frog grew more and more tired,
and Izzy's mom and dad grew more and
more impatient of waiting in the
getaway car.

"I don't know how much longer
we can keep this up, Frog,"
Izzy said...

as she finished the family portrait she'd
just painted...

and as Frog curled

Mrs. Bumble's eyelashes.

Nothing was making
the funny feeling go away.

And soon Sunnyside Lane didn't seem
quite as silent and still as it had once been.

Izzy was sure she could hear voices in
the dark, and Frog was convinced
they were being watched.

"They're on to us Frog!" Izzy shivered.
"They're going to throw us in jail!"
quivered Frog.

But when they listened more closely,
they were surprised at what they heard...

"Lawrence won best dressed at the super-duper dog show last week!"

"It's our turn, Mrs. Stevens. You got robbed last week!"

"Put the TV near the window so they can see it."

"Did you leave the front door unlocked?"

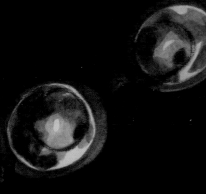

"I'd love to know how they got that gravy stain out of the sofa."

"Make sure Granny's best silver is in clear sight!"

"I wish I had
the recipe for those
brownies!"

"What's going on?"
Izzy called bravely
into the dark.

"Shh! They'll hear us!"

"WILL YOU COME AND ROB OUR HOUSE?!" everyone shouted.

"But aren't you upset about all your missing things?" asked Izzy, as the families piled out into the street.

"Oh no!" they all chirped. "We had far too much clutter anyway!"

Izzy suddenly felt very tired.

"But, I'm a burglar," said Izzy, hopelessly, "from a long line of burglars. And burglars aren't meant to be good."

Then suddenly, Izzy realized how she might be able to make the bad feeling in her stomach go away for good.

Izzy and Frog turned out to be
such fantastic burglars
that all of the families on
Sunnyside Lane wanted
them to visit...

and Izzy never
had that bad feeling
in her stomach
again.